Letterland

Bedtime Stories

By Domenica Maxted

Illustrated by the Geri Livingston Studio

This updated edition published by Letterland International Ltd, Leatherhead, Surrey, KT22 9AD, UK

www.letterland.com

10 9 8 7 6 5

ISBN 978- 1- 86209-289-1
Product Code: T41

First published 1997. New edition published 2004 by Collins Educational. An imprint of HarperCollinsPublishers Ltd.
LETTERLAND® is a registered trademark of Lyn Wendon.
Published 2008 by Letterland International.
Reprinted 2010, 2011

British Library Cataloguing in Publication Data
A Catalogue record for this publication is available from the British Library.

Designed by Susi Martin
Based on characters originated by Lyn Wendon

Peter Puppy's Perfect Pizza

One morning, Peter Puppy woke up and knew that something exciting was going to happen that day. "Wake up, Peter!" called his mummy. "It's playschool today!"

Peter Puppy lept out of bed excitedly. He was going to start playschool that morning. He would see his friends, play in the playground and learn lots of new things.

"And at snack time," said his mummy, "there'll be lots of nice things to eat."

"Will there be pizza?" asked Peter.

"I don't think so," said his mummy.

"Then I don't want to go," said Peter sulkily. "I only like pizza!"

Peter Puppy did indeed like pizza. He wanted pizza for breakfast, pizza for lunch and pizza for tea. If he was hungry in between meals, he asked for a snack – of pizza. If he went on a picnic, he wanted to take a sandwich box – full of pizza.

Peter Puppy's mummy didn't know what to do. She didn't mind him eating pizza but she did want him to try some new things as well.

"Please, Peter," she'd say. "Just try some nice potatoes, or salad, or meat. You can't eat pizza all day long." But the reply was always the same: "I only like pizza!"

So Peter Puppy's mummy decided to go and see Clever Cat and ask her what she should do. Clever Cat was having her breakfast.

"He doesn't want to go to playschool?" said Clever Cat. "Oh dear! Playschool is lots of fun. I loved school. That's how I got to be so clever."

"He doesn't want to go because there won't be any pizza," said Peter's mummy.

"No pizza?" said Clever Cat. "Now, let me think!"

Just then Harry Hat Man came by, eating a hamburger. Clever Cat told him the problem.

"Hhhmm," said Harry Hat Man, thinking hard. "I know! Let's get Peter's friends to tell him about the things they like to eat. That might change his mind."

So Peter and his mummy went to call on Noisy Nick, who was having breakfast with Eddy Elephant.

Eddy was eating a lovely boiled egg. "Try an egg, Peter," he said. "They're really good for you. And they taste excellent!"

But Peter just shook his head. "I only like pizza," he said.

Noisy Nick was eating noodles for *his* breakfast!

"Have some noodles, Peter," said Nick. "They're really nice. I have them for breakfast, lunch and tea."

"I wish he liked other things as much," sighed Noisy Nick's mummy. "Like eggs or pizza."

"I like pizza," Peter pointed out. "That's all I ever want to eat."

As they left Nick's house, Dippy Duck flew by with something round and tasty in her beak.

"Look!" said Peter Puppy's mummy. "Dippy's got a doughnut. Doughnuts are delicious."

"Bouncy Ben has been baking," shouted Dippy Duck with her mouth full. "Go and see!"

Bouncy Ben was bouncing past Clever Cat's cottage with a tray of blueberry buns. "Go on, Peter," he said. "Have one. I have just baked them."

But Peter shook his head. "I only like pizza," he said.

By now they had reached the seashore, and there stood Oscar Orange on top of a big box. "What's in the box, Oscar?" asked Peter.

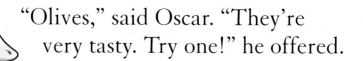

"Olives," said Oscar. "They're very tasty. Try one!" he offered.

"No thank you," said Peter. "I only like pizza."

"Have an orange," shouted an octopus who was playing in the water. "They are lovely and juicy!"

"I don't like oranges," said Peter. "I only like pizza."

Just then Sammy Snake came by on a skateboard. "What about salami?" he suggested. "Salami is so special. I just love it!"

"I don't like salami," persisted Peter. "I only like pizza."

By now, Peter's mummy was getting worried. What was she going to do with Peter? It was nearly time for playschool and Peter still didn't want to go because there wouldn't be any pizza. As they stood there, looking into the water, Walter Walrus's head popped up.

"What's the matter?" asked Walter.

Peter's mummy explained the problem.

"I've got an idea," said Walter. "On Wednesdays I'm a waiter at a very special café in town. You go to playschool this morning, Peter, and

I'll make you the perfect pizza for your lunch. What about that?"

"OK," said Peter.

So Peter went to playschool and had a lovely time. When his mummy collected him, they went to the café in the town square where there was a special table waiting for them.

"Are you ready, Peter?" shouted Walter's voice from inside, "because the perfect pizza is coming up!"

Then Walter came out carrying the most perfect pizza Peter had ever seen. It was sizzling hot and smelt delicious. Peter was hungry after his morning at playschool, so he took a huge bite.

"Well?" asked Walter.

"It's perfect!" said Peter. "What's on it?"

"Eggs, olives and salami," laughed Walter.

"You said you didn't like eggs, olives or salami," Peter's mummy reminded him.

"I do now," said Peter.

"You see," said Walter, "it's good to try new things to eat."

"Yes," agreed Peter. "From now on, I'll try lots of new things."

And to this day Peter enjoys eating all kinds of different foods. But he still likes pizza best of all!

Secrets Under the Sea

One sunny afternoon, Walter Walrus was telling his Letterland friends stories about life under the sea.

"I think that's enough stories for one day," said Walter at last. He was longing to get back into the cool water.

"Just one more story!" panted Peter Puppy.

"Tell us the one about the treasure, Walter!" said Harry Hat Man who was hovering nearby.

"Yes, do!" exclaimed Eddy Elephant excitedly.

"Very well," said Walter. "According to legend, there is a treasure chest that lies deep, deep under the sea. The treasure has a magic spell on it."

"Tell us about the spell…" interrupted Impy Ink.

"I'm trying to," went on Walter. "Well, the words of the spell go like this:

Deep under the sea in caverns cold
Lies a magical chest from days of old.
It can only be opened, so I am told,
By one who has a head of gold."

"That's me," said Quarrelsome Queen quickly. "I wear a gold crown on my head!"

"It could be me then," said Kicking King. "I've got a crown too."

"Don't be ridiculous!" snorted the Queen. "Treasure is always found by a beautiful woman. Not by a king wearing football boots."

"Oh, please," begged Bouncy Ben, "let's go and look for the treasure under the sea. Please, Walter! Will you take us?"

"I don't know," said Walter. "The sea can be very dangerous. You'll all have to have snorkels and learn how to breathe underwater."

"That's OK," said Clever Cat. "I know how to snorkel. I'll teach everyone how to do it."

So Clever Cat taught the Letterlanders how to use their snorkels and breathe underwater. It was hard work. Firefighter Fred learnt very fast because he was used to using special breathing equipment for fighting fires. But Eddy Elephant kept sinking to the bottom because he was too heavy, and Harry Hat Man kept trying to stand on his head.

Finally, Clever Cat said that they were ready and, one chilly day, Walter Walrus led the Letterlanders down to the seashore.

"Now, remember," he said. "Stay together! And if you need help, shout as loud as you can."

"All right, Walter. We're ready," said everyone.

They plunged into the sea. It was much colder than anyone had expected and Quarrelsome Queen screamed. Noisy Nick couldn't resist splashing her, which was very naughty.

"Who did that?" shouted the Queen. But Nick had already dived down under the water.

Underwater it was so beautiful that the Letterlanders forgot all about being cold. There was coral of every colour of the rainbow, and all kinds of sea creatures – whales, seahorses, crabs, lobsters and sea anemones. There were fishes of all shapes and sizes too, from fierce sharks to little stripy fish that looked like tiny jewels.

"What's this?" said Munching Mike, looking at something gleaming on the sea bed. "Is it the treasure?"

"Of course not," said Vicky Violet. "Look! It's just a bit of old seaweed inside a shell."

Suddenly, they all heard a muffled shout. "Help! Help!"

"Who's that?" asked Walter, very worried.

"It's Uppy Umbrella," called Clever Cat. "She's trapped in a bubble."

"Don't worry, Uppy!" shouted Walter. "I'll rescue you. I'll pop the bubble with my tusks."

"Be careful, Walter," said Clever Cat. "Mind you don't pop Uppy by mistake."

But Clever Cat needn't have worried. One tap from Walter's tusks and the bubble burst. Uppy Umbrella shot out, upside down. "Thanks, Walter!" she shouted.

"Over here!" shouted another voice. "Quarrelsome Queen has found the treasure!"

It was true. Quarrelsome Queen had found a beautiful golden chest. It stood inside a cold underwater cavern, just as the rhyme had said.

"Stand back!" Quarrelsome Queen cried. "I'll open it. I'm the one with a crown of gold."

But, however much Quarrelsome Queen pulled and wrenched and twisted, she could not open the golden chest. "What's the matter?" she panted at last. "Why can't I open it? It's not fair!"

"You know," said Clever Cat, "the rhyme just said head of gold. It didn't say anything about a crown."

"But that's silly. Who on earth has got a head of gold?" snapped Quarrelsome Queen.

Just then, Golden Girl came swimming towards them, her golden hair streaming out behind her.

"Of course!" said Walter Walrus. "Golden Girl has got a head of gold. A head of golden hair!"

"Go on, Golden Girl," said Jumping Jim. "Try and open the chest."

Shyly, Golden Girl swam towards the chest. She placed one hand gently on the lid and immediately it sprang open. Inside, the Letterlanders found a hoard of golden crowns, necklaces and goblets – all gleaming in a strange light.

"You did it, Golden Girl!" shouted Jumping Jim.

"What are you going to do with the treasure?" wondered Walter Walrus.

"I'm going to find out who it really belongs to and give it back," said Golden Girl. "Maybe it was stolen from a king or queen."

"Well, it doesn't belong to this queen," said Quarrelsome Queen quietly, turning away. "I couldn't even open the chest."

"Look at this, Quarrelsome Queen," yelled Yellow Yo-yo Man. "I've found something for you."

The Yo-yo Man had gone further inside the cavern and had discovered a beautiful golden throne. "There's something written on it," he said.

Kicking King came forward to read the message that was carved into the stone walls of the cavern.

> *"On this chair only a queen can sit.*
> *No-one else should even think of it.*
> *But only a queen who is of this mind –*
> *Quiet and peaceful, sweet and kind."*

"There you are, my dear," said Kicking King. "Only a queen can sit on this throne. But you have to be sweet and kind all the time. Do you think you can manage that?"

"Of course," said Quarrelsome Queen. "Aren't I always?"

At this, the Letterlanders all laughed. But Kicking King replied kindly, "Not always, my dear. But we love you all the same!"

Around the Campfire

"A holiday!" said Harry Hat Man. "That's what we need. A Letterland holiday!"

The Letterlanders were sitting in Golden Girl's garden, enjoying a picnic. They were talking about what they would like to do in the summer holidays.

"Let's go somewhere with sea and sand," suggested Sammy Snake.

"Water parks are wonderful," said Walter Walrus.

"What about a boating holiday?" said Bouncy Ben. "My brothers and I went boating last summer. It was brilliant!"

"Let's have an adventure holiday," said Annie Apple, swinging from a tree. "That would be absolutely fantastic!"

"I want to go somewhere quiet," said Quarrelsome Queen, loudly.

"Oh no!" said Noisy Nick, quietly.

"I'd like a sporting holiday," said Kicking King, "where I can practise kicking a ball every day."

"What about a motoring holiday?" said Munching Mike. "We could visit some scrap metal yards. Mmm!"

"And I could drive my ink-pen car," said Impy Ink.

"Oh no," yawned Yellow Yo-yo Man. "That doesn't sound much fun. I'd like to go sailing on a yacht."

"Wait a minute," said Clever Cat, "I've got an idea! Let's go somewhere where we can go on boats, play football, have lots of fun and be quiet too, if we want. Let's go camping!"

So the Letterlanders decided to go on a camping holiday. Talking Tess found some tents, Clever Cat collected all the cooking equipment and Sammy Snake organised sleeping bags for everyone. They found a lovely spot near a stream and put up their tents in the shade of the trees.

What a wonderful day they had! Vicky Violet and Quarrelsome Queen played in the stream, and Firefighter Fred went fishing. Kicking King flew a kite and Sammy Snake sunbathed.

Eddy Elephant was being extremely playful. He filled his trunk with water and squirted everyone.

"Stop it, Eddy!" cried Vicky Violet. "I'm soaking!"

"Don't you dare squirt that water at me!" shouted Quarrelsome Queen.

"All right." said Eddy. He squirted the water over his shoulder instead but it hit Zig Zag Zebra in the face.

"Sorry!" exclaimed Eddy as Zig Zag Zebra zoomed out of the water. "It was an accident."

"Don't worry, Zig Zag Zebra," said Talking Tess. "I will dry you with my towel."

Next, the Letterlanders played some games. They played football, baseball and tag. Talking Tess was the best at tag, although Red Robot was the fastest runner. Uppy Umbrella was so excited that she kept floating upside down in the air.

As darkness fell, they all returned to camp. Firefighter Fred made a fire and began to fry the fish that he had caught. Talking Tess hung the wet towels up to dry and Bouncy Ben began making the beds. Dippy Duck made some hot drinks and Clever Cat toasted crumpets.

It was very cosy around the camp fire. Golden Girl played her guitar and Sammy Snake told stories. The Letterlanders snuggled together and listened as the night got darker and darker.

At last, Quarrelsome Queen said, "Well, I think that's quite enough. Let's go to bed now and have some peace and quiet."

The Letterlanders began to get ready for bed. Then, suddenly, Annie Apple started to cry.

"What's the matter, Annie?" asked Golden Girl.

"I can't sleep," replied Annie Apple. "I'm scared there may be wild animals about!"

Then Uppy Umbrella started to get upset. "I can't sleep either," she whispered. "Nor can I," said Peter Puppy.

"Don't be scared," said Vicky Violet. "It's lovely and cosy inside the tents."

"But there's no light," sobbed Annie Apple. "I like to have a light on at home when I go to sleep."

"I've got a torch," said Talking Tess. "Do you want to borrow it, Annie? Max can fix it to a branch for you."

"I can't keep a torch switched on all night," said Annie Apple. "The batteries would run out."

The Letterlanders didn't know what to do. They gathered around Annie, Uppy and Peter to comfort them. All except Zig Zag Zebra, that is, who was fast asleep.

"How can we cheer them up?" wondered Walter Walrus.

"Try counting stars," suggested Sammy Snake. "That always sends me off to sleep."

"Try thinking about nice things," said Noisy Nick. "Like naughty tricks, or new toys, or noisy airplanes."

"You can borrow my special quilt," said Quarrelsome Queen. "That always helps me sleep."

"What about some cocoa?" called Clever Cat.

"Or a nice metal spoon?" mumbled Munching Mike.

But Annie, Uppy and Peter still looked unhappy. "I want to go home!" sobbed Annie.

"Don't worry, Annie," said a lovely soft voice. "I've got something that will help you."

Annie turned round. There was Lucy Lamp Light holding up her lamp. Lovely light shone all around her.

"My lamp is very special," said Lucy Lamp Light. "It will shine all night long so you never need be afraid."

"Oh, thank you, Lucy," said Annie. "We won't be scared with your lovely light shining all night, will we Uppy?"

But Uppy Umbrella was already fast asleep. Upside down, of course!

The Big Space Adventure

One morning Oscar Orange woke up to find a strange yellow light streaming through the curtains. Whatever could it be?

Oscar went to the window and looked out. He rubbed his eyes and looked again. Then his mouth opened in a big O of amazement. There was a spaceship in his garden!

Oscar went outside to investigate. From inside the spaceship came an odd sound – a sort of whimpering, whining, wailing noise. Oscar tapped on the window.

"Who's there?" he said. "Come on out!"

The only answer was a sad, "Oh, oh, oh!" from inside the ship.

"Come out!" called Oscar. "Whoever you are."

Eventually a sad little face peeped out. A sad little green face, with long antennae. It was an alien!

"Who are you?" asked Oscar in astonishment.

"My name is Splurg," said the alien. "My spaceship has broken down and I can't get home. Oh, oh, oh!" And Splurg started crying again.

"Don't worry," said Oscar. "I know just the person to fix your spaceship."

Oscar rang Fix-it Max. "Can you fix spaceships, Max?" asked Oscar.

"I can fix anything," said Max. "I'll get my box of tools and come straight over."

Max got his spanner and hammer and worked hard at fixing the spaceship. Meanwhile, Oscar took Splurg inside for an omelette and a glass of orange. After a while, Splurg began to cheer up and told Oscar wonderful stories about his home on Planet Gurtlegloop.

"All fixed!" called Max from outside. "All we need now is some spaceship fuel."

"I'll get it," called Firefighter Fred who was passing. "I'm meeting Golden Girl at the garage."

When Fred came back, they put the fuel in the spaceship. "There," said Max. "It's ready."

"That's perfect," said Splurg. "How can I ever thank you?"

"I would like one favour," said Oscar. "Could I have a go in your spaceship?"

"Of course," said Splurg. "It's just the right colour for you! But I've got an even better idea. Why don't you come and visit me on Gurtlegloop? I'd love you to see my home."

"How can we do that?" asked Max.

"With a bit of space magic," said Splurg. With this, he sprinkled some space dust on Max and, before he knew it, Max was wearing a helmet and spacesuit.

"Now you can breathe in space," said Splurg. "I

have enough space dust for all your friends. Would you all like to come to my planet for a visit?"

The Letterlanders were very excited about going into space.

"How pleased the aliens will be to see a real queen," said Quarrelsome Queen. "I'm sure they have never seen one before."

"I can't wait to travel in a spaceship," said Annie Apple. "I've always wanted to be an astronaut."

"I hope they've got a spaceship big enough for me," said Eddy Elephant excitedly. "I'd love to go on a space expedition."

Eddy needn't have worried. When he got home, Splurg sent a big rocket to collect all the Letterlanders, along with a special egg-shaped spaceship for Eddy.

Planet Gurtlegloop was wonderful. The land was purple with mighty mountains looming in the distance. All around there were small craters with aliens peeping out of them, eager to see their new visitors. The Letterlanders couldn't wait to explore.

"I love Gurtlegloop," giggled Golden Girl, zooming past on her special galactic scooter.

"So do I!" yelled Noisy Nick. "I can make as much noise as I like, and no one will tell me off for being noisy."

"I can see Letterland from here," said Talking Tess, looking through her telescope. "It's terrific!"

"Amazing!" agreed Annie Apple. "I just love being an apple astronaut."

Quarrelsome Queen was giving the aliens her most queenly wave. "Hello, Gurtlegloopers," she called. "Prepare to meet a real queen!"

Just then, there was a soft cough behind her.

"Er, Quarrelsome Queen?" said Splurg. "I'd like you to meet our ruler, Queen Blurg."

Poor Quarrelsome Queen! She wasn't the first queen in space after all. But she shook Queen Blurg's hand with good grace and said, "Thank you very much for a lovely visit."

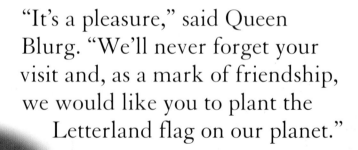

"It's a pleasure," said Queen Blurg. "We'll never forget your visit and, as a mark of friendship, we would like you to plant the Letterland flag on our planet."

So Firefighter Fred planted the Letterland flag on Planet Gurtlegloop, way out in space. And there it flies to this very day.

Putting on a Pantomime

It was winter time in Letterland. The Letterlanders were talking about their annual pantomime. Every year they put on a pantomime and everyone did something to help – acting, painting sets, making costumes or building scenery.

"What shall we do this year?" wondered Walter Walrus.

"Mother Goose!" said Golden Girl. "I'd love to dress up as a lovely white goose."

"I'd like to be a fox," laughed Firefighter Fred. "Then I could frighten your goose!"

"Robin Hood!" roared Red Robot. "I want to rush around dressed as Robin Hood!"

"I'd like to be a pirate!" piped up Peter Puppy.

"An opera singer!" said Oscar Orange.

"A dragon!" declared Dippy Duck.

"Oh dear," said Golden Girl. "However will we decide which pantomime to put on, when you all want to be different characters?"

"Unless someone writes a pantomime for us with all those characters in it," volunteered Vicky Violet.

"But who would be clever enough to write a pantomime for us?" asked Annie Apple.

"I know!" said Harry Hat Man. "Clever Cat!"

The next morning Harry Hat Man and Golden Girl went to see Clever Cat. She was sitting in her café having a cup of cocoa and doing the crossword.

"Hello, Clever Cat!" Golden Girl greeted her. "We've got a problem for you."

"A problem?" purred Clever Cat. "What sort of problem?"

Harry Hat Man sat down and put his hat on the table. "The problem is this: we need someone to write a pantomime that includes Mother Goose, Robin Hood, a fox, a pirate and a dragon."

"Don't forget the opera singer," said Golden Girl. "And Jumping Jim told me this morning that he wanted to be Jack in *Jack and the Beanstalk*!"

"Hmm!" said Clever Cat. "That will take some doing but I think I can manage it. Give me a couple of days and I'll write the pantomime."

Two days later the Letterlanders had a meeting at Clever Cat's café. Sammy Snake was eating spaghetti and Eddy Elephant was enjoying an egg. Munching Mike was moodily munching some magnets hoping no-one would notice.

Clever Cat put down her cup of cocoa and cucumber sandwich and called the meeting to order.

"Now, listen everyone," said Clever Cat. "This year the pantomime is going to be called *Robin Hood and the Beanstalk*."

"What?" exclaimed everyone.

"Isn't it meant to be *Jack and the Beanstalk*?" asked Jumping Jim.

"This is a different story," said Clever Cat firmly. "In my story, Robin Hood climbs the beanstalk and steals the giant's treasure."

"Hooray!" shouted Red Robot.

"The golden goose helps him escape. That's you, Golden Girl. But the giant's pet fox chases them. That's you, Firefighter Fred. They escape to a magical, musical island where an opera singer lives. That's you, Oscar. Then they are kidnapped by a pirate and his pet dragon."

"Please can I be the pirate?" asked Peter Puppy.

"Can I be the dragon?" asked Dippy Duck.

"Of course you can," said Clever Cat. "But then they meet a beautiful butterfly who gives them three wishes. Their first wish is to go back home; their second wish is to give the treasure back to its rightful owners…"

"Really?" asked Red Robot regretfully.

"Really!" said Clever Cat. "And their third wish is to hear some beautiful music. I thought Oscar Orange and Uppy Umbrella could sing some of their lovely songs. And that's the end."

"That's wonderful, Clever Cat!" said Walter Walrus.

"Magnificent!" said Munching Mike. "Can I help make things?"

"Of course you can," said Clever Cat. "And I thought Walter could be Wardrobe Master."

"What's a Wardrobe Master?" asked Peter Puppy.

"It's the person in charge of all the costumes," said Clever Cat. "There are lots of costumes to be made."

"Can I do everyone's hair?" asked Harry Hat Man. "I hate acting, it's too noisy, but I love hairdressing."

"That's a great idea, Harry," said Clever Cat, pleased with his suggestion.

"I've got a question. Who is to play the butterfly?" queried Quarrelsome Queen.

"Why, Bouncy Ben, of course," smiled Clever Cat. "Would you like that, Bouncy Ben?"

"Yes," said Bouncy Ben in a small voice. He didn't beam and bounce like he usually did but everyone was so excited that they didn't notice.

"Rehearsals start tomorrow," called Clever Cat. "We'll have to work very hard."

The rehearsals went well. Uppy Umbrella sang so hard that she floated up to the ceiling. Red Robot made a wonderful Robin Hood and Golden Girl was an exceptionally graceful goose. Firefighter Fred was a very fierce fox and Peter Puppy was the perfect pirate.

Only Bouncy Ben seemed sad. He wasn't his usual bouncy self and sat quietly in a corner.

"Are you all right, Ben?" asked Clever Cat. "Are you bored?"

"No," said Bouncy Ben.

"I bet you can't wait to be a butterfly!"

"Yes," said Bouncy Ben.

At last, the day came for the first performance. Everyone was very excited. Noisy Nick was so nervous that he was absolutely silent! Quarrelsome Queen was in such a quake that she was more quarrelsome than ever.

"When are we going to start, Clever Cat?" snapped Quarrelsome Queen.

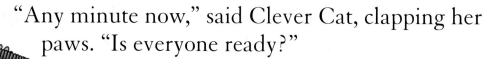

"Any minute now," said Clever Cat, clapping her paws. "Is everyone ready?"

"Hang on," said Harry Hat Man, who was brushing Vicky's hair. "Where's Bouncy Ben?"

"Ben!" shouted everyone. "Where's Bouncy Ben?"

It was Golden Girl who found him. He was curled up in a little ball, sobbing his heart out.

"Whatever's the matter, Bouncy Ben?" asked Golden Girl, giving him a hug.

"I don't want to be a butterfly!" bawled Bouncy Ben. "I want to be Batbunny!"

Golden Girl told Clever Cat, who considered the matter carefully. "Walter," she said at last. "How quickly can you make a Batbunny costume?"

"Well," said Walter Walrus, "I've got some black material left from the curtains and if someone could make a mask…"

"I can!" said Munching Mike. "I love making masks."

"Then all we need to do is find a shirt with a bat on it."

"I've got one," sniffed Bouncy Ben. "That's what gave me the idea."

"Very well," said Clever Cat. "Robin Hood and the goose can be saved by Batbunny. It makes a more exciting ending anyway."

"Brilliant!" beamed Bouncy Ben, bouncing right up in the air. "Thank you, Clever Cat. You're so clever."

The Letterland pantomime was a great success. Everyone cheered Robin Hood and the goose, and booed the pirate.

"Look behind you!" everyone shouted, as the dragon sneaked up behind Robin Hood. "Oh no, you don't!" they shouted, as the fox tried to catch the goose. But the biggest cheer of all was when Bouncy Ben as Batbunny came on stage to save the day!

Quarrelsome Queen's Questions

Can you find a picture of...

1   Annie Apple as an astronaut?

2   Bouncy Ben in a boat?

3   Clever Cat cooking crumpets?

4   Dippy Duck with a doughnut?

5   Eddy Elephant eating an egg?

6   Firefighter Fred dressed as a fox?

7   Golden Girl playing her guitar?

8   Harry Hat Man eating a hamburger?

9   Impy Ink in an ink-pen car?

10 Jumping Jim on a journey underwater?

11 Kicking King flying his kite?

12 Lucy Lamp Light with a lamp?

13 Munching Mike eating a magnet?

14 Noisy Nick making a noise in space?

15 Oscar Orange as an opera singer?

16 Peter Puppy as a pirate?

17 Quarrelsome Queen with her quilt?

18 Red Robot dressed as Robin Hood?

19 Sammy Snake on a skateboard?

20 Talking Tess with a telescope?

21 Uppy Umbrella asleep upside down?

22 Vicky Violet with a violet in her hair?

23 Walter Walrus underwater?

24 Fix-it Max in an extra-special spacesuit?

25 Yellow Yo-yo Man on a yacht?

26 Zig Zag Zebra zooming out of the water?

The Letterlanders

Annie Apple	Bouncy Ben	Clever Cat	Dippy Duck	Eddy Elephant	Firefighter Fred

Golden Girl	Harry Hat Man	Impy Ink	Jumping Jim	Kicking King

Lucy Lamp Light	Munching Mike	Noisy Nick	Oscar Orange	Peter Puppy

Quarrelsome Queen	Red Robot	Sammy Snake	Talking Tess	Uppy Umbrella

Vicky Violet	Walter Walrus	Fix-it Max	Yellow Yo-yo Man	Zig Zag Zeb

Letterland

Child-friendly phonics

The Letterland system teaches all 44 sounds in the English language through stories rather than rules. There are resources to take children from the very first stages of learning to full literacy.

ABC Trilogy

Handwriting Practice

My First & My Second Activity Books

Sticker & Activity Books

Picture Books

Games & Puzzles